Sheltie™

Rides to Win

Look for these SHELTIE books!

Sheltie™
Rides to Win

Written and illustrated by **Peter Clover**

ALADDIN PAPERBACKS

New York   London   Toronto   Sydney   Singapore

To John Thorne

First Aladdin Paperbacks edition June 2001

Copyright © 1998 by Working Partners, Limited
First published 1998 by Penguin Books Limited U.K.
Created by Working Partners, Limited

ALADDIN PAPERBACKS
An imprint of Simon & Schuster
Children's Publishing Division
1230 Avenue of the Americas
New York, NY 10020

The text for this book was set in Sabon
Printed and bound in the United States of America.
2 4 6 8 10 9 7 5 3 1

Library of Congress Catalog Card Number: 2001089102
ISBN 0-689-84182-5

Chapter One

Emma quickly finished her breakfast. She spread a glob of butter on her toast and crammed it into her mouth.

"For goodness' sake, Emma!" said Mom. "Slow down or you'll choke."

"Sorry, but I'm in a hurry," said Emma. "I'm meeting Sally at nine-thirty and I'm already late."

"Well, I'm sure Sally will wait five minutes. Now, slow down!"

Mom raised one eyebrow as she spoke. That meant there was to be no argument. Emma gave a big sigh and settled down. She couldn't help feeling excited. She had felt that way ever since she first saw the poster two days earlier.

One of Emma's favorite things to do with Sheltie, her little Shetland pony, was to sit in the saddle holding the reins loosely in her hands and let Sheltie lead the way. She liked to see which way Sheltie wanted to go and enjoyed being taken for a ride.

Two days ago Sheltie had chosen to cross the stream. First he clip-clopped over the little stone bridge. Then he walked on and stopped farther along at the village green, right next to a big colorful poster pinned to the village bulletin board.

There was a picture of a pony on the poster, and Emma read the words:

Emma had never felt so excited in her life. And that was why she was rushing through breakfast.

Emma was meeting Sally and together they were going to ride into town and put their names down on the entry form for the show. They wanted their names to be the first two on the list. Emma shivered with excitement just thinking about it.

After breakfast Emma bounded down the garden path. Sheltie blew loudly through his nostrils and dashed around the paddock in a wide circle. His eyes shined brightly as Emma gave him a peppermint treat.

"Now, no messing around, Sheltie," warned Emma. "I want to get you tacked up and off. Do you understand?"

Sheltie nodded his head, then playfully decided to pull at Emma's T-shirt.

Ten minutes later Emma and Sheltie were trotting down the lane on their way to meet Sally and Minnow.

Sheltie whinnied and flicked his tail from side to side when he saw Minnow up ahead.

Minnow was a larger pony than Sheltie. He was black and white, with a long white mane. Sheltie and Minnow were the best of friends.

Minnow gave a loud whinny in reply, as if to say, "Hello, Sheltie. We're here."

Sally greeted Emma with a big grin. "I'm so excited," she said. "I hardly slept a wink last night."

"Neither did I," said Emma. "Nothing like this has ever happened in Little Applewood before. It's our big chance to show everyone what Sheltie and Minnow can do."

Chapter Two

Emma and Sally were a little disappointed when they arrived at the village green. Alice Parker and her two snooty cousins, Melody and Simon, were the first in line.

These days Emma was quite friendly with Alice Parker at school. Alice hadn't always been very nice. She used to make fun of Sheltie and call him names. That was before Sheltie had rescued Alice from a cliff top in Summerland Bay and things had changed. Now Alice and Emma smiled and spoke to each other.

But her two cousins, Simon and Melody, were much worse than Alice had ever been. They looked down on everyone and were always cheating and playing mean tricks on people.

Sally glanced at Emma and made a face. She knew Alice's cousins too. Sally remembered her first day at school, when Melody had pulled her hair and then stood there with Simon, laughing. Sally didn't like them one bit either.

Sheltie looked around. He hadn't met the other three ponies before, and he sniffed and nuzzled in a friendly way. Alice Parker's pony was called Blue. He was happy to be friends with little Sheltie.

But the cousins' ponies! Well, they were as stuck up and as snooty as their owners.

Mrs. Linney sat behind a table on the village green. The registration book was spread out in front of her. Raising funds for the Redwings Horse Sanctuary was Mrs. Linney's idea. She had organized the entire pony show.

Mrs. Linney looked up and smiled when she saw Emma and Sheltie. She was very fond of both of them. In fact, Mrs. Linney used to take care of Sheltie before Emma moved to Little Applewood.

Alice Parker and her two cousins registered their names and entered all six events in the show.

"I bet Melody and Simon think they'll win all the events," said Emma.

"They've got to beat us first though!" said Sally.

As the cousins rode off, Alice smiled at Emma. But Melody and Simon didn't even look her way.

"Come on," said Melody. And Simon followed, leading their ponies away as quickly as possible.

Now it was Emma and Sheltie's turn. Sheltie lunged forward and knocked the registration book off the table. Then he pushed his nose close to Mrs. Linney's face and tried to lick her cheek.

"Oh, Sheltie!" laughed Mrs. Linney. "You never change, do you?"

Sheltie blew a fat, noisy raspberry, and Emma giggled.

"Have you chosen which events you

want to enter?" asked Mrs. Linney.

Emma looked at Sally and grinned.

"Yes. We want to enter everything too! But we don't want to compete against each other, because we're friends. We'd like to divide up the events and enter as a team. We're going to call ourselves the 'Saddlebacks.'"

Mrs. Linney smiled. She was only too happy to enter both girls as a team. After all, it was supposed to be a fun day, not a real competition. Mrs. Linney thought there would be a few others who would want to do the same.

"The Saddlebacks it is, then," she said. "I've put you down for all six events: the egg-and-spoon race, the potato race, the flag race, the bending course, the obstacle race, and the best show-pony contest."

Mrs. Linney told Emma that the special trophy for the winner with the most blue ribbons was to be a silver statue of a pony.

Emma and Sally made up their minds there and then that the Saddlebacks would try their hardest to win that trophy.

Mrs. Linney wished them both luck and

handed them two sponsorship forms. The next job was to find willing sponsors to donate money toward the Redwings Horse Sanctuary.

It wasn't fair for both Emma and Sally to ask the same people for donations, so the two girls decided to split up.

Emma's first stop was Mr. Crock, who was in his vegetable garden. As they trotted down the lane, Sheltie peered over all the stone walls. He liked sticking his neck into people's yards.

However, when they got to Mr. Crock's cottage, there was a surprise waiting for them. Alice Parker's cousin Melody was standing in the garden talking to Mr. Crock.

Simon was holding Sapphire's and

Midnight's reins and waiting out in the lane. When Sheltie saw them he let out a terrific snort. Simon wasn't holding the reins tightly enough and the two ponies were so startled that they pulled free and began to trot away. Without Melody and Simon in their saddles to stop them, the two ponies disappeared down the lane.

Chapter Three

The cousins were furious.

"Look what your stupid pony has done!" yelled Simon.

Then Melody said something rude to Emma and called Sheltie a big hairy ape.

Sheltie shook his mane and watched the snooty pair chase off down the lane after their ponies.

"Funny pair, those two," said Mr. Crock.

"Some nerve too. Wanted five dollars each for taking part in some charity race."

Emma explained all about the Little Applewood pony show that Mrs. Linney was putting on.

She told Mr. Crock how friends and family were sponsoring riders in various events. And how all the money collected was going to the horse sanctuary.

"There's even a special trophy for the rider who wins the most blue ribbons," said Emma.

"Well," Mr. Crock, "that explains it much better. I didn't trust those other two. But you and Sheltie, well, that's a different matter. Sheltie is worth five dollars of my money any day," he said. "But you make sure he wins those blue ribbons!" Then he signed Emma's form and gave Sheltie a carrot.

Emma's next stop was Marjorie Wallace and her brother, Todd. It had been a little while since Emma and Sheltie had come to visit. Both Marjorie and Todd were very fond of animals and only too pleased to see Emma and sponsor her in Little Applewood's first pony show.

Mudlark the donkey came up to the fence and gave a loud bray when he saw Sheltie.

"Oh, look," said Marjorie. "Mudlark has come to wish you both luck."

Sheltie gave one of Mudlark's long ears a lick, and the little donkey nuzzled him, happy to see his friend again.

The rest of the morning proved very

successful. By lunchtime Emma had fifteen names on her sponsorship form.

Emma was feeling very pleased with herself. And Sheltie seemed to be more excited than ever at the thought of being in a pony show.

☆ ☆ ☆

Later that afternoon, when Emma met up with Sally, they discussed their training plans.

"We've only got one week to get Sheltie and Minnow up to scratch," said Emma.

Minnow would probably have been ready to enter the show the following day. But Sheltie! Well, Emma thought he needed quite a bit of work.

It wasn't as though Sheltie wasn't as clever as Minnow. Sheltie was very clever. Sometimes he was too clever.

Sheltie did everything that Emma asked him to do. The difficulty wasn't in getting Sheltie to *do* certain things. It was getting him *not* to do certain things. Or worse still, getting him to *stop* doing them, particularly when he was in one of his naughty moods.

But Emma hoped that with a little practice, Sheltie would be ready to prove to everyone that he was the best pony in the show.

Chapter Four

The next day was bright and sunny. It was Sunday, and Emma could hear the church bells in the distance as she skipped down the garden path and fastened the strap of her riding hat under her chin.

Sheltie was waiting patiently by the paddock fence.

"Oh, no!" said Emma, when she saw him. "Just look at you!"

Emma could see that Sheltie had been

rolling in the paddock. His coat was covered in dry, dead grass. Several twigs were still hanging from his mane.

"Oh, Sheltie. What am I going to do with you?"

Sheltie took a nibble at the padlock and chain. Already he was frisky and ready for some fun.

"Mrs. Linney is coming this morning, Sheltie. And now it looks as though I've got to tidy you up first!"

Emma climbed over the gate and began pulling the twigs and grassy briers from Sheltie's coat. Sheltie thought this was great fun and tried to pick the flowers on Emma's sweater with his teeth!

But Emma wasn't in the mood for joking around. She was determined to clean

Sheltie up before Mrs. Linney arrived.

Emma ran to fetch a brush and a hoof pick, along with Sheltie's saddle and bridle, and worked hurriedly to have him tacked up and looking presentable.

Sally arrived on Minnow minutes before Mrs. Linney pulled up in her battered old car. As usual, Minnow was perfectly groomed, with every hair in place.

Mrs. Linney clambered out of her car and gave Emma a wave.

Emma unlocked the gate and held on to Sheltie's reins while Mrs. Linney carried a bundle of bamboo canes from the trunk of her car into the paddock.

Sheltie was eager to greet both Minnow and Mrs. Linney. He blew a series of loud snorts then nudged at the bamboo bundle in Mrs. Linney's arms as Emma closed the gate. Mrs. Linney almost dropped the whole pile.

Mom and Dad came down from the cottage with little Joshua and watched as Emma and Sally helped Mrs. Linney to mark out a course with the bamboo canes. She poked them into the ground three feet apart in a long, straight line.

"Okay!" said Mrs. Linney. "First the bending course. What you have to do is to walk Sheltie through the line of canes, weaving in and out of each one without touching any. Take your time and make Sheltie work for you, Emma. You too, Sally. Make Minnow walk slowly in and out of the canes."

Sheltie went first. He was very good at

this even though he had never tried it
before.

Sheltie didn't touch one cane until he
came to the end. Then he deliberately
pushed his nose forward, grabbed the last
marker and pulled it clean out of the
ground.

"Never mind, Emma. Leave it to Sheltie!" said Mrs. Linney. "But that was an excellent first attempt."

Minnow was also good at this event. He was a larger pony, so he wasn't as quick as Sheltie. But he did finish the course without knocking any markers down. Or pulling any out!

Sheltie's second attempt didn't go very well at all. He could weave through the markers quite easily. But now he thought the best part was pulling out the canes. This time he removed three.

Mom turned to Dad and smiled. "Sheltie is funny, isn't he?" she said. "He knows perfectly well what he's supposed to do. He just likes messing around. Poor Emma. She's going to have her hands full."

Emma whispered a few words in Sheltie's ear. After several more attempts he finally grew tired of pulling out the canes and concentrated on weaving in and out beautifully.

The first time he made a perfect run Emma gave Sheltie a peppermint. This seemed to make a lot of difference. Suddenly Sheltie could fly through the markers without touching a single cane.

But Emma agreed with Sally. Minnow might be more reliable on the bending course. Sheltie couldn't really be trusted not to play.

Chapter Five

Next Emma and Sally had some fun with the egg-and-spoon race. Mrs. Linney had brought along two hard-boiled eggs to practice with.

"On the day of the show," said Mrs. Linney, "the eggs won't be boiled, so they'll have delicate, fragile shells."

It wasn't as easy as it looked either. Riding along with an egg balanced on a spoon was pretty tricky, especially at a fast pace. And each time Emma's egg fell to the ground, Sheltie tried to roll it around and play with it.

But Sheltie did have a really fast walk, and Emma's hand was very steady too, so Sally agreed that Sheltie would do better than Minnow in this event.

After the egg-and-spoon race they practiced the flag race. This involved picking up flags from the ground, then dashing with them one at a time at a mad gallop to an empty bucket about fifty yards away.

Sally and Minnow were really fast and very good at this race. Sally was happy to have this as one of her events.

The potato race was similar. The difference was that in this race you needed to dismount to pick a potato out of the bucket.

Sheltie didn't like eating potatoes, so he left them alone. But he did manage to kick a bucket over twice. However, being a little Shetland pony, he was nearer to the ground than Minnow. And this gave Emma better aim. Emma could also mount and dismount quicker.

Sally agreed that the potato race should be one of Emma's events.

"I've never seen anyone get on and off a pony so fast!" said Sally. "I'm tired out just watching you."

All this practice was thirsty work. Dad made some iced tea and poured three drinks for Emma, Sally, and Joshua.

Sheltie and Minnow were nibbling at the grass beneath the shade of a tree when suddenly Sheltie looked up. He stared right

across the paddock out onto the road.

Sheltie was interested in something.
Emma glanced over to where he was looking and saw Melody and Simon. They were
spying through a gap in the hedge.

When they saw Emma looking over,
they kicked their ponies on and trotted
away up the road.

Emma turned to Sally and said, "Did you see those two?"

"Who's that?" asked Dad.

"Alice Parker's cousins. They were spying on us."

"Don't be silly, Emma," said Mom. "They were probably just out for a ride and were interested in what you were up to."

"Spying," mumbled Emma under her breath. She didn't trust those two and neither did Sally.

When they had finished their drinks, Mrs. Linney explained the obstacle race and the best-show-pony contest.

"The obstacle race is exactly that," said Mrs. Linney. "A series of obstacles, a bending course, and small jumps, with some tricky hazards along the way. Like walking through a clothes line of flapping towels, treading over a sheet of black plastic, or passing a brightly painted trashcan.

It sounded very easy to Emma, but some ponies didn't like surprises or things that flapped and rustled in the wind.

Emma knew that Sheltie would be great at this. Nothing scared Sheltie. He was the bravest pony in the world.

Minnow was more timid than Sheltie but would be ideal for the best-show-pony contest. After all, Minnow was a proper show-pony and Sally was an excellent rider.

By the time Mrs. Linney left, the two girls had worked out the races and events that would suit Sheltie and Minnow best.

Sheltie and Emma would compete in the egg-and-spoon race, the potato race, and the tricky obstacle race.

Sally and Minnow would take the bending course and the flag race, and enter the best-show-pony contest. Everything was settled nicely.

All that remained was a week of practice.

Chapter Six

After school on Monday, Sally rode over on Minnow to practice with Emma and Sheltie. They set up the bending canes that Mrs. Linney had left for them to use and practiced for an hour.

Although the bending course wasn't one of Sheltie's events, Mrs. Linney said there would be some bending canes set out as part of the obstacle race.

Mr. Crock had given Emma a sack of

potatoes to practice with for the potato race.

"Those potatoes won't even be good enough for french fries after you've finished with them, Emma," laughed Mom.

"They'll make good mashed potatoes though," said Emma. Her aim was improving, and she found that if she tossed the potatoes into the bucket gently, without throwing them too hard, then they didn't bounce out again.

Sally and Minnow were getting really fast in the flag race too. Minnow's quick turns were perfect for this event.

Emma was still practicing with a hard-boiled egg for the egg-and-spoon race. She knew it was going to be more difficult on show day, with a fresh egg, but Mom had said, "I'm sorry, Emma. I can't spare a dozen eggs each night just for practice."

But she did help Emma set up some small jumps and obstacles. She laid out plastic sheets and things for Sheltie to step over in preparation for the obstacle race. But Mom wasn't too pleased when Emma opened the paddock gate and started practicing in the yard, with her clean laundry hanging on the line.

Sheltie liked the way the shirts and towels flapped around his head as he dashed through them. But then he got tangled up in the laundry with a shirt sleeve wrapped around his head.

"Emma! Tell Sheltie to stop doing that!" Mom yelled from the kitchen window as Sheltie pulled a T-shirt right off the line.

"Tomorrow I'll hang out a line of old towels for you to practice with," said Mom. "But until then, leave my laundry alone!"

Melody and Simon had ridden over once again. This time they'd brought their ponies right up to Emma's backyard fence.

Melody sneered and looked down her nose as she said, "You don't think you stand a chance of winning anything on that little scruffbag, do you?"

Emma was upset.

"Don't take any notice," said Sally. "They can't see past their own stuck-up noses. Sheltie's beautiful and everyone else who knows him thinks so too!"

Emma brightened a little. Yes, she thought. Sheltie is cute and clever, and on Saturday they would show Melody and Simon just how good he really was.

Emma took a deep breath. "If you're so confident then why do you keep spying on us?"

It was Simon's turn to sneer now. "Just thought we'd check out the competition," he said. "But we can see now that we don't have any!"

Then he dug in his heels and turned his pony, and they both trotted away.

Chapter Seven

The next evening, after school, Sally came over again as planned. This time they practiced together for the best-show-pony contest. Even though this was going to be Sally's and Minnow's event, Emma and Sheltie joined in.

First, they walked around the paddock. Then they trotted around in a perfect circle, keeping close to the fence. They practiced walking forward for six steps, then stopping before walking backward.

"Walking backward is tricky, isn't it?" said Emma.

At first Sheltie kept going backward too fast, and Emma found it difficult to make him stop after six steps. Minnow, on the other hand, did exactly what Sally asked of him.

"You'll soon get the hang of it, Emma." Sally leaned forward and rubbed Minnow's neck.

They practiced turning tight circles. Then they practiced standing absolutely still without moving. Sheltie was great. Normally, he couldn't stand still for long without fidgeting and jangling his reins. But he had been training really hard and stood perfectly still for fifteen seconds.

Even when a bumblebee buzzed around his head, Sheltie didn't move. He just watched it until it flew away.

"Well done, Sheltie!" said Emma. She felt so proud of him and leaned forward to give him a kiss.

Emma couldn't wait to show Melody

and Simon just how wrong they were about Sheltie.

The rest of the week passed really quickly, with one hour's training every afternoon after school.

On Friday evening, the night before the pony show, Emma didn't feel like eating anything at all. Butterflies danced in her tummy and she felt sick.

"It's probably nerves," said Mom. "You're just worrying too much about tomorrow." She tucked Emma up in bed nice and early to get a good night's sleep before her big day.

Emma lay awake for ages. Every time she closed her eyes she kept seeing Melody's and Simon's snooty faces.

What upset Emma most, though, was that they thought Sheltie couldn't do anything because he was small. And that they laughed at Sheltie because his coat wasn't smooth and shiny like their ponies'.

Emma didn't care about that. She liked Sheltie's rough, shaggy coat and his long tail and mane. Still, she decided to get up extra early in the morning and give Sheltie a really good grooming.

Emma finally went to sleep thinking of Sheltie and dreamed of him galloping free with his mane blowing in the wind.

Chapter Eight

In the morning Emma leaped out of bed, crossed to the window, and drew back the curtains. It was a beautiful, bright sunny day. A perfect day for a pony show.

Sheltie was standing in his usual spot by the paddock gate. Emma could see from the window that Sheltie had been rolling in his straw. A big clump of it was stuck to his forelock, right between his ears. Sheltie looked funny, as though he

was wearing a straw sunhat.

Emma laughed and felt all tingly inside. She hugged herself to keep the excitement from bursting out. Then she got dressed quickly in jeans and a T-shirt before making her bed and rushing downstairs.

As soon as Emma opened the kitchen door and looked out, Sheltie became frisky. He did a little stomping dance, then shook his head, tossing his mane so hard that the straw flew off in a shower of golden strands.

Emma had at least one hour before breakfast time to get Sheltie ready. First his coat and then his tail and mane.

Sheltie seemed to know that it was a special day and was on his best behavior. For once, he stood absolutely still and seemed to enjoy the grooming as much as Emma did. He even let her put on his hoof oil without a protest.

By the time she had finished, Sheltie looked neat and tidy, with a handsome, floppy forelock and bright, shiny hoofs.

Emma fed Sheltie his breakfast, then raced back to the cottage for her own. But before she did she gave Sheltie a stern warning: "NO MORE ROLLING!"

Everyone seemed to arrive at the town green together. A tent had been set up and a huge banner was strung between two trees. LITTLE APPLEWOOD PONY SHOW was painted across the banner in bold red letters.

Beneath the canopy was a long table which held the winners' ribbons and the impressive silver trophy. Mrs. Linney sat at the table with a long list of competitors' names in front of her.

Mrs. Fairbright, the vicar's wife, was

also there alongside Mr. Price, who was Emma's principal at school. They were both wearing big badges that said JUDGE on their lapels.

Emma leaned forward and gave Sheltie's thick neck a good hard pat. Sheltie was interested in everything going on around him and wanted to make friends with everyone.

Emma felt very sophisticated in her navy blue riding jacket and white jodhpurs. Mom had bought the jacket specially for Emma to wear at the show. It was second-hand and the sleeves were a little too long. Emma had to roll them up a bit, but she didn't care. She felt like a proper horsewoman.

Sally had on a blue riding jacket too, so

they looked like a real team. Emma felt certain that the Saddlebacks would do really well.

As Emma and Sheltie waited in line to sign in with Mrs. Linney, Emma looked around at the other riders and people at the show.

She saw Mr. Crock, and Marjorie and Todd Wallace. She saw Alice Parker on her pony, Blue, and gave her a wave. Alice mouthed "Good luck" and Emma gave her a nod and grinned. She also spotted Melody and Simon and quickly looked away.

Mom and Dad were there. Joshua was sitting high on Dad's shoulders and waved both hands like a windmill as soon as he caught sight of Emma and Sheltie. Emma beamed him a big smile, then blew him a kiss.

Suddenly Emma and Sally were next at the front of the line.

It took some time for all the riders to sign in. But soon everyone was ready, and Little Applewood's first pony show was about to begin.

Chapter Nine

"Will all riders in the egg-and-spoon race take their positions, please." Mrs. Linney's voice boomed through a megaphone and called the competitors to the waiting area at one end of the green.

Everyone whose name was called walked their pony up to the starting line. There turned out to be too many to run in one race, so the contestants were divided into two groups.

Melody and Simon were together in the first group. Emma and Sheltie were in the second group with Alice Parker and Blue. The first five ponies to finish up in the first group would race against the first five from the second group.

Each of the riders was given a spoon and a nice fresh egg. The first group of contestants stood in a neat line with their eggs balanced on their spoons waiting for the starting signal.

Mrs. Linney swished a flag and they were off!

Ten ponies raced down the length of the village green at a fast walk. The crowd yelled and cheered as eggs got dropped and smashed. Riders grinned with excitement as they urged their ponies forward toward the finishing line.

Melody and Simon were in the lead. Melody's pony, Sapphire, was really fast. She was almost trotting, yet the egg stuck to Melody's spoon as though it were glued.

Emma was amazed. It was going to be very difficult to beat Melody and Simon. Then, just before the finishing line, Simon's egg popped out of his spoon and smashed on the grass.

He was out of the race, and Melody took first place on Sapphire.

Ten more ponies lined up at the start. They were given eggs on spoons and waited for Mrs. Linney's flag.

Emma was feeling pretty nervous and had to concentrate really hard to keep her spoon steady.

Mrs. Linney swished her flag and the race was on. Alice Parker and Blue were the first away.

Sheltie only had short little legs but he could move them really quickly. Sheltie's fast walk was almost the same speed as his trot.

There were three other ponies ahead of him, and Sheltie started to walk faster and faster.

Then Blue went over a bump and Alice's egg leaped out of her spoon. Emma held her spoon steady as Sheltie put on a final spurt and crossed the finishing line in third place.

That meant that Emma and Sheltie would be racing again against Melody's Sapphire and eight other ponies.

"You were fantastic," said Sally. "Sheltie was going like a rocket!"

Emma smiled, but inside her tummy the butterflies were dancing again. The truth was she felt more nervous than ever when she lined up again for the final race. She patted Sheltie's rump and concentrated on holding her spoon steady.

Emma and Sheltie were standing next to Melody and Sapphire. Melody sat with her spoon at arm's length and looked down at Emma with a smug expression.

"You might as well give up now, with shorty," she said, looking at Sheltie with a horrible sneer. Emma took no notice, but Sheltie did. Without any warning he tossed his head sideways and knocked the spoon out of Melody's hand.

The strange thing was that, as it fell, the egg stayed in the bowl of the spoon. And the egg didn't break when it hit the ground either. It stayed in the spoon as it lay on the grass.

Mrs. Linney took two steps over and bent down to pick up the spoon. She'd seen what had happened. Melody's egg was hard-boiled, and there was a little blob of chewing gum sticking it to the bowl of her spoon.

Mrs. Linney put both the egg and spoon into her pocket and handed Melody another spoon and a fresh egg. She raised her eyebrows as she looked straight at Melody and said, "Try again with these, dear."

Melody's face turned bright red.

Emma smiled to herself and whispered, "Good job, Sheltie," under her breath.

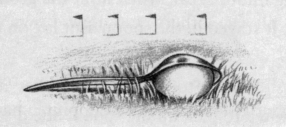

Chapter Ten

Emma and Sheltie stood at the starting line.

The flag swished and all the ponies shot forward. Melody and Sapphire were away in a flash. And so were Emma and Sheltie. The two ponies streaked away from all the others and flew down the green.

Sheltie's little legs were moving really fast. But Melody's pony, Sapphire, had a much longer stride, and soon Melody was in the lead.

"Go, Sheltie!" yelled Sally. "Go, Emma!"

Sheltie was now neck and neck with the larger pony. The finishing line approached. Sheltie stormed past in first place, with Emma still balancing the egg on her spoon. Sheltie had won!

Melody threw down her spoon. Her egg smashed on the grass as Mrs. Linney announced through the megapohone: "The winner is Emma Matthews on Sheltie, riding for the Saddlebacks."

Emma felt so proud. She leaned forward and gave Sheltie a big hug.

"You think you're really clever, don't you?" Melody snapped at Emma. "You and shorty were just lucky, that's all."

"We won fair and square," said Emma. It was her turn to be smug now, and Emma enjoyed every minute of it.

Mr. Price looked very pleased when he pinned a winner's blue ribbon to Sheltie's bridle.

"Well done, Emma," he said. "And well done, Sheltie."

Sheltie looked across at Melody and blew a loud raspberry. Melody made a face and stuck out her tongue.

The next event was a bending course. This event was set against the clock, with points lost if any of the markers were touched.

Sally and Minnow did really well, but took second place to Simon on Midnight.

"Never mind," said Emma. "You did your best. And you were both great."

Sally smiled. She felt really pleased even though she hadn't won.

Next was the potato race and, by this time, Sheltie was eager to have another turn at something.

As before, there were two rounds, and once again Emma and Sheltie found themselves in the final roundup against Alice Parker and her two cousins.

Alice seemed to be enjoying the show. But Melody and her brother Simon kept whispering together and staring over at Sheltie. They gave Emma the creeps. She didn't like either of them one bit. And neither did Sheltie.

The winner of the potato race would be the first rider who tossed five potatoes into their empty bucket.

Everyone had a bucket full of potatoes at the starting line. Empty buckets sat twenty yards away ready for the potatoes to be dropped into them. This was Emma's favorite event.

At a swish of Mrs. Linney's flag the race began.

Sheltie was in great form. He seemed to be going at a hundred miles an hour. All Emma's potatoes went straight into her bucket. Other riders were not so lucky. Potatoes were bouncing everywhere. And with everyone running around, it was difficult to know who was winning.

Emma had four potatoes in her bucket already and was just about to drop in a fifth when she heard Melody shout, "I've won!"

Mrs. Fairbright blew a whistle and everybody stopped.

Emma couldn't believe it. None of her own potatoes had missed, yet she was certain that she had seen at least two of Melody's go bouncing out of her bucket. Emma thought that she had been well ahead of Melody.

Sheltie seemed to think so too. He was staring at Melody and making loud snorting sounds.

Melody was laughing and looking at Emma with her arms raised up in the air. Emma looked down into Melody's bucket. There were five potatoes there, all right.

But Sheltie couldn't stop staring at the sleeves of Melody's riding jacket. One of them looked particularly lumpy.

When Melody finally lowered her arms to receive the winner's blue ribbon, Sheltie decided to take a better look. He grabbed hold of Melody's sleeve and gave it a tug. And out popped two potatoes for everyone to see. They bounced onto the grass at Mrs. Fairbright's feet. Melody had been cheating again!

Emma was the only rider with four potatoes in her bucket. So the blue ribbon was given to Emma instead.

Mrs. Linney had a quiet word with Mr. Price and Mrs. Fairbright. Then they called Melody over on Sapphire.

"If you can't play fair, Melody, I'm

afraid you will be disqualified from the show," said Mr. Price.

Mrs. Linney stepped in. She looked very stern and said, "We've decided to give you one last chance, Melody. So just behave."

Melody made a face, then kicked her heels and stormed off on her pony.

As she passed Emma, Melody hissed. "It's your fault, Emma Matthews," she said. "I'll get you for this!"

Chapter Eleven

The pony show continued.

The next event was the flag race. Straightaway Melody was up to her tricks again. She kept deliberately crossing in front of Minnow and confused Sally by dropping her flags into Sally's bucket instead of her own.

Then Melody starting yelling, "You're a cheater, Sally Jones!"

Everyone heard and this made Sally mad.

Although she tried really hard and made a terrific effort, Sally only managed to finish in second place. Simon won the race on Midnight. That meant he had won two races and was now equal with the Saddlebacks.

"I can't believe that Melody," said Emma. "She cheats at everything."

"I know," agreed Sally. "But she's really sneaky, isn't she? She made that one look like it was my fault."

"We'll have to keep an eye on her, won't we, Sheltie?" said Emma. Sheltie nodded his head then shook out his mane with a snort.

Almost all the riders would participate in the obstacle race.

The most difficult part was getting the

ponies to walk through the flapping towels on the clothesline and across the rustling plastic. Most of the ponies shied away and took fright. One pony absolutely refused to go anywhere near either obstacle.

Emma spoke gently in Sheltie's ear. She knew that Sheltie could do it. She told him so. Sheltie was fearless.

Now it was Emma's turn. So far the best time for completing the entire course was two minutes and twenty-eight seconds.

Mrs. Linney swished her flag and Sheltie went into action. First he stepped nimbly over six striped poles that lay on the grass. Then he cleared three small jumps and turned at a marked tree.

Next they had a quick canter to the bending course. In out, in out, in out, in—

Sheltie stopped for a second and looked at the last cane.

"Don't you dare," said Emma as she squeezed with her legs. Sheltie hurried on and left the cane alone. "Phew!" breathed Emma, relieved.

They raced on to the dreaded black

plastic sheet, but it was no problem for Sheltie.

Emma was a little worried about the clothesline. She thought Sheltie would be tempted to tug at one of the towels. "Please, Sheltie," Emma whispered. "No joking around."

But Sheltie was having so much fun that he didn't need to mess around, and he passed through without even a glance at the flapping towels.

Sheltie took another jump over a small bale of hay, then trotted past a fearsome looking trash can tied with balloons, and dashed straight past the finishing line.

Sheltie and Emma had clocked the fastest time yet!

"One minute, thirty seconds," screamed Sally.

Emma felt so proud. Sheltie blew through his lips and snorted, tossing his mane and holding his head high in the air.

"Your time is going to be hard to beat," smiled Sally.

In fact, no one else came close until it was Simon's turn.

Simon and Midnight were riding last. It seemed almost impossible, but they clocked exactly the same time as Emma and Sheltie.

The judges decided to award both Sheltie and Midnight a blue ribbon. That meant that both Emma and Simon had three ribbons each in the competition for the special pony-show trophy.

There was only one event left to go. Sally and Minnow were up against Simon and Midnight for the best-show-pony contest. It was up to Sally and Minnow to win the final blue ribbon to secure the special trophy for the Saddlebacks.

Poor Sally was feeling nervous.

"Just do your best," said Emma. "It won't be the end of the world if we don't win the trophy, Sally. But it would be nice to beat Simon."

"I know Minnow can win, Emma," said Sally. "I just wish I could shop shaking!"

"Just pretend that you're practicing in the paddock," suggested Emma. "You were fantastic yesterday. Try to forget the crowd and concentrate really hard."

Sally smiled and sat up straight in the saddle.

Then disaster struck. As Sally walked Minnow over to the arena he stumbled and put his foot in a hole. When he pulled his foot out, he had lost a shoe.

"Oh, no!" said Sally.

Emma rushed over on Sheltie to see what had happened.

"I don't believe it," said Emma. "Minnow won't be able to compete now!"

Emma held Minnow's horseshoe in her hand, and Sally looked tearful. She was so disappointed.

"I'm sorry, Emma," said Sally, trying not to cry.

"It's not your fault," said Emma. "It

could have happened to anyone. But what do we do now?"

There was only one answer: Emma and Sheltie would have to step in at the last moment and take their place.

"You and Sheltie can do it, Emma," said Sally. "I know you can."

"It's the standing still part that I'm worried about," said Emma. "We've been training really hard, but Sheltie has never had to do it in front of all these people."

But Sheltie was their only chance.

Simon looked over and gave a nasty sneer. Then he laughed when he saw Emma holding Minnow's shoe.

Melody was standing next to him. Simon whispered something to her and she disappeared into the crowd.

Chapter Twelve

Only eight ponies were entering the best-show-pony contest as it was such a difficult event. The ponies needed to be extremely well-behaved and would be asked to perform various exercises.

Mrs. Linney pulled the riders' names out of a hat to decide who would go first. Simon and Midnight were picked to perform seventh. Emma and Sheltie were drawn eighth—the last in the event.

Emma drew a deep breath. Eight was her favorite number.

Emma and Sheltie had to stand and watch all the other riders compete before them. She grew more and more tense.

Sally stood with Emma while the other riders went forward.

"Waiting around is the worst part, isn't it?" said Sally.

Emma nodded. "It seems to be taking forever."

Even Sheltie was getting restless. He jangled his reins and stamped his hoofs.

Then suddenly Sheltie became very interested in the overhead branches of a nearby tree.

"Oh, do keep still, Sheltie. Please!" Emma spoke softly, and Sally gave him a piece of carrot to keep him quiet.

Finally it was Simon's turn on Midnight. Mrs. Linney started the clock and called out.

"First complete a neat, tidy trot in a wide circle around the arena."

Midnight held his head high and looked like the perfect show-pony.

"Now take six steps backward between the two bales of hay," continued Mrs. Linney. "Then take six steps forward and turn a tight circle." Midnight did both of these very well.

After that there was a figure eight walking normally, ending with fifteen long seconds of standing still.

Finally, Midnight jumped over six poles, cantered to a blue marker, and stopped in front of the judges' table.

Simon and Midnight scored thirty-three points. This was by far the best score in the competition.

Emma took a long gulp. "That score is going to be hard to beat," she said.

"I know. But if anyone can do it, you and Sheltie can," said Sally.

Then it was Emma's and Sheltie's turn.

Mom came over and gave Emma a hug. "Good luck, Emma. Just do your best!"

The crowd hushed to silence as Emma and Sheltie walked into the arena.

Emma's heart was beating really fast as she took up her position and Mrs. Linney set the clock.

Sheltie's circle in trot was perfect. He held his head proud and lifted his little legs high. The light breeze caught his long

mane and it billowed out to the side.

Then Sheltie took six nervous steps backward between the two bales of hay, followed by six confident steps forward and turned a perfect tight circle.

"Go, Sheltie!" someone shouted. "You show them!" It sounded like Mr. Crock.

Emma grinned with pride.

Next was the figure eight and standing perfectly still for fifteen seconds. This was the part Emma was dreading.

Emma counted the seconds. She only got to four when suddenly there was a loud bang. It seemed to come from high in a nearby tree.

Sheltie pricked up his ears.

Please don't move, thought Emma. Then she heard the sound of a branch snapping.

Before Emma could do anything to stop him, Sheltie charged forward and rushed over to the tree.

"Oh, no!" cried Sally.

Sheltie stood beneath the tree and looked up into the branches to where the sound had come from.

Emma looked up too, and what she saw made her gasp. Melody was high in the tree clinging to a broken branch. It looked very dangerous. Melody was about to fall at any moment!

Chapter Thirteen

Dad came rushing across the grass as Emma slipped out of the saddle.

"Quick, Dad," said Emma. "It's Melody."

"Hold Sheltie still," said Dad as he climbed up onto Sheltie's back. He stood on the saddle and reached up to help Melody.

"Somebody get a ladder!" he called.

Sheltie was wonderful. He kept absolutely still and didn't flinch or move a

muscle. One slip and both Dad and Melody would come tumbling down. Dad was able to support Melody's legs, but he didn't think the branch would hold much longer.

Then, just in time, someone arrived with a ladder. Melody screamed as the branch finally broke away and crashed to the ground.

Luckily, by then Melody was already on the ladder, and Mr. Price was helping her down.

The crowd cheered and Sheltie blew a ripple of noisy snorts.

"What were you doing in that tree, young lady?" asked Mr. Price.

"Nothing," said Melody, even though she had climbed up the tree and popped a paper bag to scare Sheltie. But her plan had backfired and Sheltie had ended up saving her!

Melody was so embarrassed at being caught that she burst into tears and ran away.

Because Sheltie's turn in the contest had been interrupted, he was allowed to start again.

This time Sheltie performed all the exercises perfectly. Even the standing still part. All those hours of practice had really paid off.

There was a long silence as the points were totaled. Emma held her breath.

"Oh, Sheltie. Do you think we've done enough to win?" whispered Emma in Sheltie's ear.

At last Mrs. Linney announced: "Emma and Sheltie riding for the Saddlebacks have scored thirty-four points. The winner of the blue ribbon is Emma Matthews on Sheltie."

The noise was deafening. Whistles and cheers rang in Emma's ears. She had never felt so happy or so excited in her entire life.

Sheltie pawed the grass as Mr. Price

pinned a blue ribbon to his bridle.

"We're so proud of you both," he said, beaming a big smile. "Well done."

Then a special announcement was made.

"The winners of the Little Applewood pony-show trophy are the Saddlebacks!"

Sally walked Minnow into the arena and joined Emma and Sheltie.

"Isn't it fantastic?" said Emma.

"We won," said Sally. "We really won!"

"And we beat snobby Simon and Melody fair and square. That was the best part," smiled Emma.

The Saddlebacks received the special silver trophy. It was a pony galloping with its mane blowing in the wind.

"We can share it," said Emma.

Then they held the trophy between them and lifted it up in the air.

Alice Parker came over with Simon. She was pulling him by the arm. Simon just stood there. Then Alice gave him a nudge and he thanked Emma and Sheltie for rescuing his sister.

"Great job, Saddlebacks," he added.

The words seemed to stick in his throat.

Sally's father joined them in the arena. He was so thrilled about Sally and Emma's victory that he took out his checkbook and gave an extra donation to the horse sanctuary.

Now that the pony show was over, Sheltie was back to his naughty self. He lunged forward and snatched the check from Mr. Jones's hand.

"Don't you dare eat that!" said Emma.

Sheltie blew a noisy snort, which sounded like a laugh, and his eyes sparkled with mischief as only Sheltie's could.